CONTENTS

THE GOLDEN RING

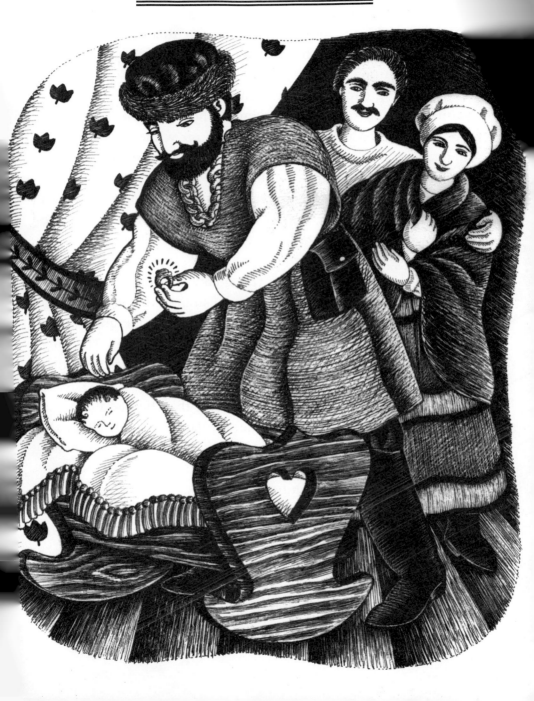

-re was once a king who had no children of his own. As the *ars* passed, he and the queen longed more than ever to hear the *aughter* of children in the castle and, of course, they needed an heir to the throne.

One spring day, when the scented lime trees were lush after warm rains, the king was returning to the castle with two of his troopers. He ordered his men to ride on while he paused to meditate in the countryside. The troopers were reluctant to let the king out of their sight, but they were obliged to obey him.

The king dismounted and breathed in the fragrance of the land which, in his busy life, largely went unnoticed. He crossed the grass to a dense spinney where a carpet of bluebells spilled out to the tufted grass at its edge.

Wearily, he ventured into the dusky world. It took some moments for his eyes to become accustomed to the change of light. Small rodents scampered nervously in the undergrowth and startled birds moved to higher branches or flew away. The king walked on, stumbling over gnarled roots and marvelling at all that was new to him.

He was so engrossed, he stayed longer than he had intended. By the time he was ready to ride on, darkness had fallen. He thought he was retracing his steps, but in fact he was moving further away from the spot where he had dismounted. Soon it became obvious to him that he was lost.

"If I keep moving, it is logical that I must meet someone sooner or later," he said to himself and endeavoured to walk in what he hoped was a straight line.

Before long, he emerged from the trees and found himself in scrubland. Ahead, half hidden in a clump of bushes, was a dwelling with candlelight flickering through the open door. From within came the sound of laughter and music. "Surely someone here will set me on the right road for the castle?" he thought.

Not knowing who these people were and having no wish to reveal his true identity, the king slipped the gold ring from his finger and placed it in the pocket of his tunic. He thrust his fine, leather gloves inside his boots and approached the doorway.

He had arrived at the home of a poor family who were celebrating the birth of their baby son. The king, looking like a tired and dusty traveller, was welcomed in immediately by the baby's father.

"Welcome, sir. Come and share our refreshments," he said kindly. "My home is yours. It's not often we see a solitary traveller in these parts after dark."

The king sat down and the baby's mother and father brought a plate of pork, dumplings, freshly-baked rye bread and honeycake, as well as a tankard of mead. The king was grateful for the food and drink. Soon his feet were tapping to the fiddler's music. Throughout this, the baby managed to sleep peacefully in the corner as though he heard nothing at all.

Later, as the last of the guests left for home, the couple offered the traveller refuge for the night.

"It is not wise to be abroad till daylight, sir," said the man. "Wild things move about here in the night. Better you wait here until the dawn. Although we have little to offer, you are very welcome."

The king, who had been well-protected all his life and had never journeyed alone, was relieved to hear that he could stay.

"We can only offer you old sheepskins to lie on," said the mother. "But at least they are clean and warm. As you see, we are poor people."

The couple brought in the sheepskins and spread them on the floor. Then, taking the baby, they went to sleep in another area. The weary king wrapped himself in the skins and was soon asleep.

At morning light the couple prepared a large pot of porridge with fresh milk. The king ate hungrily and it was only then that he asked directions to the royal castle. "It is there I was bound when I became separated from my companions," he said, still not wishing to reveal more.

In the light of day the couple could see the fine leather of the traveller's tunic and believed they had given shelter to a rich nobleman. When the traveller bent over the baby's cradle, they were amazed at the thick gold chain that was revealed, glistening round his neck. But what the traveller said was more surprising: "What is the name of your new baby?"

"Mirek, like his father," said the mother fondly. "Now I have two Mireks."

"You are very fortunate. Mirek is a beautiful baby," said the traveller. "My wife and I have no children. You have shown me much kindness; it would please me to be of help to your son. I would like to educate him when he grows to boyhood and, if he is diligent and responds, he will have a chance to learn all that wise people can teach. He will grow to be a fine gentleman of whom you will be proud."

The parents did not know what to say. The traveller certainly had a proud bearing and rich clothes, but they knew nothing more of him. They could not possibly entrust their son's life to a complete stranger.

They were shaking their heads when the king drew the gold ring from his pocket. The moment they saw the engraved royal crest, the couple knew the traveller was none other than their king.

At first they were speechless, then flustered and embarrassed. "Your Majesty! Sire! Oh, we didn't know, truly!" cried the man, falling to his knees. "How could we know? We have glimpsed you only from afar."

"You honour us with your presence in our home," said the woman with a deep curtsey, thinking with shame of the king sleeping on the floor in an old sheepskin.

"Now, now, there is no need for alarm," said the king with a smile. "You knew only what I wished you to know. And you were quite right to refuse my offer to help your son. But in view of my identity, would you reconsider my offer?"

Well, of course, the parents knew that it was quite a different matter now. They agreed readily. The king placed the ring in the baby's cradle and said: "This is for Mirek alone. Guard the ring carefully. When he is fourteen, he is to wear it and present himself to me at court. From then on, I will do all I can for him. Rest assured, he will come to no harm in my castle and he will not lose touch with you. When the time is right, you will see him again."

The man then led the king on foot until the turrets of the castle could be seen. "I know my way from here," said the king, "I was not as lost as I thought."

"No, Sire. It is the darkness that plays tricks."

"I bid you farewell," said the king. "As you see, already I am found. We will meet again."

No sooner had the king started across the grass than a troop of horsemen appeared, cheering loudly. They surrounded the king and knelt on the grass. Calls of "Sire! Sire!" told the poor man that indeed he had been with his monarch.

He watched for a few moments and pondered: "Aye, he may be the king, but by tomorrow all thoughts of my Mirek will have gone from his head." Then he went home to his wife and son.

As the years passed, Mirek grew to be a healthy, handsome boy with the quiet courtesy of his parents. His father often spoke to him of the night the king came to stay and he took Mirek whenever he could to see the king in the distance, but never once did he mention the king's offer or the ring which he had hidden away.

On Mirek's fourteenth birthday, his father produced the ring from its hiding place in the mud floor of their home and gave it to his son. He repeated the king's words and, though it was hard for Mirek to understand, he knew he would do exactly as he was told. The golden ring was too big for the boy's fingers so they bound it with flax to make it fit.

"Do not part with it ever. That is a royal command," said his father. "The ring is for you alone. You are to go straight to the castle and do the king's bidding in all things and we will be proud of you, my son."

"I shall not disappoint you," said Mirek. "I will learn all my tutors can teach me and one day I hope to be of service to the king."

His parents had made him a new woollen shirt and trousers and had given him a fur-trimmed tunic and hat and the best leather boots they could afford. With a little food in a linen bag, Mirek was ready to go. His father wanted to accompany him at least half of the way, but Mirek wished to go alone.

The longest part of his journey was forging a way through the spinney which was now as dense as a forest. When the sun became hot overhead, Mirek sat down for a rest and a bite to eat. As he tore his bread apart, he suddenly heard the snapping of twigs behind him.

Jumping to his feet, he was just in time to avoid a figure that threw itself in his direction. A youth of about his own age, but coarse and fierce, stood with feet astride, brandishing a cudgel.

"Give it here," he said savagely, snatching the bread from Mirek's hands. "What else you got?"

Mirek took a piece of meat from his bag and that too was snatched from him. Within minutes, the ruffian had swallowed all the food. As he wiped his mouth on his grubby arm, he noticed the ring on Mirek's finger. "Oi! What's this then? What you doing with this, eh?"

So far, Mirek had not said a word. Now he said: "It's a ring. My father gave it to me."

"A ring, from your father?" said the boy doubtfully. "Very likely, I'm sure. Give it here."

Since Mirek had been told not to part with the ring, he refused.

"Wha-at! You dare say no to me? You better give it here quick, or else!" said the ruffian. He raised the cudgel above his head, but Mirek did not flinch. Instead of hitting him, the youth dropped the weapon and grabbed Mirek's hand. There was a violent tussle, but Mirek held on until the flax binding came undone and the ring slipped from his finger.

Once he had it, the youth bit on it with his yellow teeth. He declared it to be solid gold.

"Your father gave you this, did he?" he jeered. "Next you'll be saying you're the son of rich parents. You with your home-spun clothes! You're nothing but a thief – like me. You stole it. Come on, own up."

"No I didn't. I'm not a thief," said Mirek indignantly. "I tell you my father gave it to me. And I want it back." He lunged at the boy's hand but was thrown off-balance by a fist like a rock. He fell backwards on to the ground. The coarse fellow leapt at him. They struggled and fought among the bracken until Mirek, who was no match for the hefty youth, was pinned down.

"Now tell the truth and all of it," snarled the boy.

So Mirek told the story of the king's visit and how he was on his way to the royal castle. The youth turned the ring round and round on one finger. As he listened, his sly, conniving expression suggested he was hatching a plot.

"If you want me to spare your life, you'll do as I say," said the boy, giving Mirek a final shake. "The ring is mine now. I'm the one who's going to the king and you are my servant. Is that clear?"

"No, never, never!" shouted Mirek, kicking the ground with his heels. "You have no right to … " – but his protests were lost as the youth dragged him to his feet and reached for the cudgel.

"My friend here says yes. You do what I say!"

Mirek saw there was no way out. He would have to agree.

"All right! All right! I'll do as you say," he gasped, thinking that when they reached the castle the truth could be told.

The youth insisted they change clothes since Mirek's garments were better than his. But the clothes were too small for the fellow and he could hardly cram his feet into the leather boots. Mirek, however, had no trouble getting into the dirty, ragged clothes which were much too big for him.

"Oi! Something else. What's your name then?" asked the boy.

"Mirek. What's yours?"

"Zig. Big Zig they call me. And you're my servant. Don't forget it." The youth waved the cudgel in front of Mirek's face then threw it into the undergrowth and gripped Mirek by the arm

They made an odd couple as they went on their way and eventually came to the castle gates. Although the guards were surprised to hear that the boys had come to see the king, they recognised the royal ring and the two were admitted. The ruffian was taken at once to the king's chamber while Mirek was sent to the servants' quarters.

The king and queen were dismayed by the boy's rough appearance and the cheeky way he strutted into the room. Although fourteen years had passed, the king remembered the man and his wife with their gentle and courteous ways. This fellow bore no resemblance to either of them. He could not speak properly and he did not even bother to bow. Yet there was no doubt it was his own golden ring which he had placed in the baby's cradle, although he could no longer remember the baby's name.

Food was ordered as an expression of hospitality and the royal couple looked on as the boy pushed everything into his mouth at once, until it was stuffed like a pouch. Even the guards turned their eyes to the roof.

"Perhaps you should send him home again," whispered the queen. "I doubt that he will ever fit in at court. Admit your mistake and let us be done with it. I fear we may have trouble with him."

But the king did not wish to break his promise to the boy's parents so it was decided that Zig should stay. They would see what could be done with him.

Zig made his home at the castle. He was given fine clothes, a comfortable room, lessons every day and good food. Mirek was dressed in servant's livery and instructed to see to his master's needs.

As the weeks went by, Mirek's eyes turned often to the horizon. He wished his mother and father might come to visit him, then the king would learn the truth. But the couple were awaiting contact which the king had assured them would be made when the time was right. They knew they could not invite themselves to the castle.

Mirek had hoped for an opportunity to speak with the king, but it did not happen. The castle was huge and there was no way of meeting him by chance.

As for Zig, he was given the title of Prince and became an abominable show-off, as well as being rude. He learned neither good manners, nor any of the lessons his tutors set him. At the same time, he could see how nimbly Mirek's brain worked. He attended the lessons to be of service to his master and it was clear how quickly he understood all that was taught. His popularity with everyone sent Zig into vicious tantrums. He feared that one day Mirek might attempt to reveal the truth and the king would believe him.

Zig resolved to rid himself of Mirek.

Often there were banquets at the castle to which brave knights were invited and with them came tales of quests, battles and great valour. Prince Zig listened to these thrilling and frightening tales and soon discovered how he could send Mirek away for ever.

A story was told of a certain well many miles away in a wilderness which was said to hold the clearest, most health-giving water in the world. At the bottom of the well was a heap of treasure. Many brave knights had gone in search of the treasure, but few had returned. There were those who boasted that they had almost secured it, but it was doubtful that they had ever tried.

Prince Zig saw this as a way of sending Mirek to his death, since he was unlikely to succeed where the bravest in the land had failed. He sent Mirek off with nothing more than a few provisions in a knapsack, convinced that he would never return.

Mirek followed the route the knights had described, but unlike the tales, he met no danger of any kind. At last he came to a wide, barren landscape where few trees grew and only a tumbledown hovel showed that someone had once lived there. The well was, as he had been told, in the middle of nowhere but it was not guarded by any of the monsters he had been led to expect.

By now, Mirek's waterbottle was empty and, longing for a cool drink, he approached the well and looked down into it. The water was transparent and sparkling, but there was no bucket with which he could draw it up. He was wondering what to do when he saw a movement out of the corner of his eye. From the tumbledown hovel, an old man emerged in a long brown robe. His grey beard reached almost to his waist.

"Good day, sir," said Mirek, "I didn't think there was anyone about."

"And good day to you, young man. Have you come to drink from my well?" inquired the old man.

"Oh, I'm sorry. I didn't know it belonged to anyone," said Mirek in surprise. "I have been sent here by my master."

"Your master, the prince?" asked the old man, although Mirek had not said so.

"How did you know?"

The old man smiled mysteriously into his beard. "Many things can be heard on the wind, if you have ears to hear," he said. "You are the first one who has come here asking for water. All others come for the treasure they see at the bottom of the well."

"I didn't notice any treasure, sir," said Mirek truthfully, since he had been anxious only for a drink.

"You speak the truth. You did not look with greedy eyes," said the old man knowingly. "This is a well of unfathomable depths. Please, you are welcome to take all you need."

"But sir, there is no bucket. I –" Mirek stopped as the old man held out a length of very slim rope.

"Tie this to your waterbottle and lower it," he said.

Mirek did so and was surprised that the water level was much further down than it appeared to be. When he had quenched his thirst, he filled the bottle in readiness for the return journey and prepared to go when the old man spoke again. "I have a word of warning for you, young man. Your master does not expect your return. When he sees you, he may send you on yet another quest. Remember to take this piece of rope with you."

"Yes sir. Thank you," said Mirek. "But what shall I do with it?" He was thinking the rope was too thin to be of much use.

"You will put it in your knapsack. The rope is as strong as the water is clear. I made it myself. Remember, take it with you. May you return safely to your master."

When Zig saw Mirek he was furious and angrier still that he had not brought the treasure.

"I saw none," said Mirek who realised that the treasure was in the imagination of those who sought it. "The water was crystal clear, but I saw no treasure."

Zig did not believe he had gone to the well at all and immediately set him another task. He was to go to the mountain cave of a woman called Janna; she was holding for ransom Princess Wanda from a neighbouring country. Janna was known to be fiercer than the brigands who had their dens in the mountains and had a cunning beyond compare.

As before, Mirek was sent with no means of defence and only a few provisions. His route lay through a high mountain range whose summits were lost in the clouds. When he reached the foothills, no one he spoke to would talk of Janna or say where her cave could be found. Mirek walked about the mountain paths for weeks. The only caves he saw were empty, save for birds which fluttered out as he drew near.

Then one clear, moonlit night he came upon a sheer rock face like a sheet of glass. High above was a black space which appeared to be the opening of a cave. There was something so forbidding and eerie about it that Mirek was sure he had found the dwelling place of Janna. Around the entrance were large, jagged rocks like the fangs of animals guarding the interior. There was no way of scaling the smooth surface of the rock. Mirek knew he had to take Janna offguard before dawn – if she was there. But how could he do it without a foothold?

Just then a light breeze blew by and it reminded Mirek of the old man at the well. The old man had warned him to take the rope and Mirek had forgotten about it. He had put it in his knapsack as he was told and he had not touched it since. It should still be there.

Swinging his bag from his shoulder, Mirek thrust his hand inside. The rope was there, coiled up at the bottom. Mirek withdrew it. He did not think it would be much help, yet the old man had assured him of its strength. Mirek tied a lasso loop and tossed the end upwards to the jagged rocks at the mouth of the cave. Again and again he tried, until the rope looped itself over the stoutest rock. If the old man spoke the truth, the rope would bear his weight, if not, he would crash to his death down the mountainside.

Gingerly he began to climb, entwining his legs to hold the rope steady. Up and up he went and the rope did not stretch or fray.

At last he reached the mouth of the cave. Whether it was the home of Janna or some wild beast he would soon find out. Pushing the rope back into his knapsack, Mirek was ready to go in.

Testing the ground ahead with his toes, since all was black, he moved slowly forward. From somewhere deep inside came the sound of birds calling in agitation. "It is not Janna's cave after all," thought Mirek. He was just about to turn back when his arms were seized by unknown hands and he was hustled forward further into the cave. Rounding a curve, he saw torches blazing on the walls and sitting on a high chair like a throne was a strange woman with her arms folded across her chest. From the shadows cast by the torches, her sharp features could be seen, but her eyes were in the shade – like two dark holes in her face.

"Bring him close," she said in a voice that sent shivers down Mirek's spine.

The huge, glaring eyes seemed to blaze brighter than the torches. "What are you doing in my cave?" she asked. "And how did you get here?"

Mirek knew he had to be bold. He had to face her with a bravery he had never had to summon before. If she sensed his fear, all would be lost. He drew a deep breath.

"I have come for the Princess Wanda," he said firmly. "I shall not leave without her and I will not tell you how I came."

Janna rose to her feet and towered above him. As she raised her arms, a scarlet cloak billowed behind her and laughter echoed horribly round the cave. It seemed to rattle Mirek's bones.

"And what will you give me in exchange?" she asked at last.

"Nothing at all!" replied Mirek, clear as a bell.

The eyes widened even more, then narrowed to slits. "You are not like the snivellers I have seen before. You are brave and bold. I like that. Bravery is a challenge. This is what you must do. You will choose the princess's pet bird from among many others. If you choose correctly, you take the princess and go. If you choose wrongly, you remain here with me."

"Anything you say," said Mirek at once, but rashly.

The woman led him to a chamber in the cave where many birds flew about in a wide cage. Their brilliant feathers shone like rainbows. Mirek had never seen such magnificent birds and guessed they must have come from afar.

"Which one is the princess's pet bird? You have but a few moments to make up your mind."

Mirek's eyes were dazzled by the display. The sleek gloss and sharp look of each beauty as it swooped in front of him seemed to implore him to choose it alone. Mirek raised his hand again and again, ready to point. Almost out of sight at the back of the cage, huddled a small brown bird. It did not fly. Its head drooped on its chest.

"That is the princess's bird," cried Mirek, pointing confidently. "That is the bird I choose."

Janna seemed at once to shrivel where she stood. "How could you know? How did you guess?" she hissed.

"I do not have to answer you," said Mirek triumphantly. "That was not part of the bargain. Now you must keep your word. Set the princess free."

To Mirek's surprise, Janna kept her word. She brought from another part of the cave a young woman with a pale, thin face and long blonde hair the colour of the flax that had once bound the golden ring. Although he had never seen her before, Mirek had no doubt that this was Princess Wanda. The small brown bird was released from the cage and came to perch happily on her shoulder.

"Go!" screamed Janna. "Leave my cave at once! But if you falter on the way, you will be mine."

Mirek took the princess's hand and ran with her to the mouth of the cave. Quickly, he looped the rope over the same stout rock and they began to slide down it together. He was startled to hear the harsh laughter of Janna echoing after them. She had not given up. Then a huge red bird seemed to fill the entrance above. It was Janna hacking at the rope to send them to their deaths. She sliced and whacked frantically, but the rope did not break.

By the time Mirek and the princess had reached the cliffs below, Janna had given up and gone raging back into the cave. Mirek jerked the rope from the rock and thrust it into his knapsack. So far, they were safe.

They hurried down the mountain paths and clambered over the rocky foothills. The rest of the journey would surely be easy. The night was clear and starry with a high moon that gave a clear view of the countryside. But as they began to walk on the flat ground of the plains, a high-pitched screeching filled the air. It was painful to the ears. Thousands of bats appeared in the sky – flying so close together that the light of the moon was obscured. Janna was tricking them into losing their way and giving up. Mirek was afraid he would take the wrong direction and they would be lost.

"Do not be alarmed," said the princess in a quiet voice. "My bird knows the way. She will take us to the castle where I spent

happy days as a child."

Although the bats followed them throughout the night, the little bird flew ahead without wavering. By daylight the bats had gone and before long Mirek and the princess were crossing the grasslands that led to the castle and safety.

When the lookout on the tower saw them coming, the news spread rapidly throughout the castle. The gates were opened and people ran out to greet them. It had been known that Zig had sent his servant on a hopeless quest and no one -- least of all Zig -- expected to see Mirek again.

They were cheered all the way to the king's chamber where Mirek was astonished to see his mother and father. They could bear the silence no longer and had come to seek news of their son. The king had recognised them immediately as the couple who had given him shelter more than fourteen years before, but he had no good news to give them of their son. That is until the moment he appeared.

The castle was scoured for the rascally Zig but he was nowhere to be found.

As for Mirek, he took his rightful place at the castle, became since Mirek and married Princess Wanda. The king gave the gold ring back to Mirek. As he had said when the baby was born, the ring was for him alone.

Mirek's parents went home to live contentedly in their little house beyond the spinney and their son came to see them as often as he could.

ZIK, ZAK AND MATHEW

There was once a farmer who had three sons who were triplets. Zik and Zak were sharp-witted and knew how to make life easy for themselves. Mathew was quiet and did most of the work on the farm to help his father.

Mathew was up every morning before dawn and had milked all the cows long before his brothers had stirred in their sleep. At the end of the day, he was the last to go to bed after securing the animals for the night. The farmer urged Zik and Zak to work harder and give Mathew a rest, but they would not change their ways.

One severe winter, the farmer spent many days on the cold, snowy hillside mending cattle fences. When he returned, he became ill and died. Immediately, Zik and Zak looked about for their father's will, anxious to know who had inherited the property. They searched every corner of the house, but found nothing.

"It's usually the eldest who inherits everything, isn't it?" said Mathew, trying to be helpful.

"Of course it is, stupid!" snapped Zik. "But we're triplets, so which one of us is the eldest?"

"Take no notice of him," said Zak. "What does he know?"

Zik and Zak were sure their father had saved money in his lifetime and they were determined to find it. Since it was not in the house, they took spades and dug deep holes in the land until the animals had scarcely a safe place to tread. Still they found neither will nor money.

After that, they went about whispering, planning to get rid of Mathew and share everything between themselves. They called Mathew into the kitchen and pointed to a hook on the wall where their father's old working clothes still hung.

"Those are for you, brother," said Zik. "Father must have left them for you in his will, only we can't find it."

"Get a bite to eat and off you go," said Zak roughly. "Two mouths are enough to feed here. Without money, we can't all stay on the farm."

"But where shall I go? How can I earn a living?" asked Mathew, not quite understanding what they meant.

"Go where you like," said Zik. "You haven't enough wits to run a farm without father. We'll take care of it. You find somewhere else to live."

Mathew knew he was no match for his brothers and did not argue. He took his father's clothes down from the hook and put on the old jacket which was too big for him. There was also a pair of threadbare trousers which he wrapped up in a cloth together with some bread. Then he left his home. He wondered what would happen to the animals since his brothers had never cared for them before.

Mathew wandered across the fields he knew so well and stopped to drink from the stream at the boundary of their land. As he was scooping the water up in his hands, a swallow darted down from the sky and came to rest on a stone in the stream.

"Don't look so sad, Mathew," said the bird in a soft, chirping voice. "Your father did not forget you."

Mathew, who was almost in tears, looked up and blinked. "What do you mean, pretty bird?" he sniffed.

"I mean that your father was a wise man," said the swallow. "He understood your selfish brothers very well. He knew they would turn you out with nothing but rags."

"And so they did," sighed Mathew. "Father was quite right. But how does that help me?"

The swallow flew off the stone and alighted on the grass close to Mathew. "I know a wonderful secret," it whispered. "I can tell you, now that you are away from your brothers." Mathew began to shake his head, but the swallow went on. "Your father left you all his wealth, Mathew. It is sewn into the lining of the old jacket you are wearing. A small fortune goes with you on your back. Spend it wisely and your father will rest in peace."

Before Mathew could reply, the swallow had spread its wings and soared into the clear sky. Mathew pulled off his father's jacket and tugged at the lining. The stitches came away easily and he put his hand into the space.

It was true. Little cloth bags had been sewn inside the jacket and Mathew realised at once why the jacket had seemed so heavy. His fingers trembled as he opened one of the bags. Inside was a solid gold coin. The jacket was lined throughout with gold pieces. He was wise enough not to disturb the rest of the gold. Putting the jacket on again, he made his way to the country lane and began to walk briskly away from the farm.

He went, not knowing where to go or what to do with his sudden wealth.

"The only thing I know about is farming," he said to himself. "I think I'll buy a farm with a good bit of land and work as I did before."

He walked about the countryside for most of the day. It was almost dusk when he came to a small white farmhouse that was for sale, together with three good-sized fields. Mathew bought it and within a few weeks he had stocked it with the finest animals and grain his money could buy. He worked long hours each day, falling into bed exhausted when darkness came.

A few years later, he had the most successful farm in the neighbourhood. For the first time in his life, Mathew was happy.

But before long, Zik and Zak heard about their brother's thriving farm and one day they came driving by in their shabby cart to see it for themselves. It was all they had been told. Rich crops filled the fields and well-cared-for animals grazed in the pastures. They could not believe it belonged to their brother until they saw him by the farmhouse.

"Hello there, brother! How well you're looking," called Zik, with a forced smile.

"You've happened on good times then," said Zak, jumping down from the cart.

Mathew, who bore no grudge against his brothers, invited them into his house. He gave them pasties filled with sauerkraut and mushrooms and brought out a bottle of mead wine to celebrate.

Zik and Zak rolled their eyes in circles as they looked jealously at their brother's home. Then they turned on him with anger in their eyes.

"You must have found father's money," snarled Zik.

"Yes and you didn't tell us," stormed Zak. "None of this is yours. It really belongs to us."

Mathew was so shocked he could think of no reply. He ran out into the yard, but they followed him. Zik took a rake, Zak grabbed a brush and together they began to beat their brother.

"Clear off, you little thief!" shouted Zik. "And don't come back or it'll be the worse for you!'

Mathew found himself being pushed out through the gate of his own property and it was closed behind him. "You can have the old farm," Zak yelled after him. "It's good enough for the likes of you."

So, for the second time, Mathew was turned out of his home. But this time he did not have a penny on him. He took the road that would lead him back to the old farm and did not reach it until well after dark.

As he came near, the animals that remembered him – the cows, the horses and even the hens – set up a joyful noise for their one true friend.

But Mathew hardly knew his old home. The windows were broken, there were holes in the roof and the door hung loosely with its lock missing – and this was not all. When dawn spread over the countryside, Mathew saw the animals – thin and neglected. Field after field choked with weeds. He sat down and moaned with despair. But the animals came to him nudging and murmuring as though begging him not to give up. So Mathew resolved to start all over again.

It was hard work. Sometimes at the end of the day he was too tired to cook his supper and went to bed hungry; but he persevered. Slowly, the farm came back to life. It seemed to Mathew that he would be content to stay there for the rest of his life.

One day in summer as he was walking in the cornfield, he heard someone crying on the other side of the hedge. Climbing over the gate, he saw a young girl weeping bitterly. "Hello there! What troubles you?" he called. "Can I be of any help?"

"I-I'm l-lost and I don't know what to do," cried the girl, her face streaked with tears.

"Tell me where you live and I'll take you home," said Mathew kindly. But the girl cried all the louder.

"I l-live in Krakov," she sobbed.

"Krakov?" Mathew repeated. "Surely not. That's at least four days' journey from here."

"I know, but it's true," said the girl, drying her eyes at last. "My name is Danuta. I've been travelling with my parents. We were going home when we stopped the carriage to change horses. I jumped out and hid – just for fun – and the carriage went off without me. I ran and ran but I can't find the carriage anywhere."

"I'm not surprised," said Mathew. "You've run a long way from the carriage road. This is only a farm lane."

When she heard this, Danuta began to cry again. Mathew reassured her. Taking her home, he gave her a bowl of potato soup and beef dumplings. Afterwards, he drove her to the home of a merchant who had a daughter of Danuta's age. The merchant promised to look after Danuta until her parents came to find her.

Every week, Mathew went to visit her taking little gifts from the farm. Sometimes it was a cream cheese, sometimes a basket of big brown eggs and always he took an armful of wild flowers from the hedgerow.

A year went by and still Danuta's parents had not come to look for her. Mathew became very fond of her and made up his mind that if her parents had not come by Easter, he would ask Danuta to marry him.

The following spring, on Easter Monday, Mathew packed a hamper with special Easter cakes and drove off in his cart to the merchant's house. But Danuta had gone. The merchant told him that a richly-dressed lady and gentleman had come and claimed Danuta as their daughter.

Mathew was desolate. He was so unhappy he drove the longest way home, to pass the time. It was midnight when he reached the farm and he was startled to see the lamps were lit.

Someone was in his house.

When he opened the door, Mathew saw his brothers' coats hanging on the pegs. Although the lamps were burning, his brothers were not in sight. Silently, Mathew tiptoed through the house and found his brothers tucked up in his bed.

"What are you doing here? Why are you in my bed?" Mathew was so annoyed that he shouted – probably for the first time in his life.

Zik and Zak sat up, rubbing their eyes. "Why, you young scoundrel, how dare you ask us that!" growled Zik, still half asleep.

"You're a villain and a rogue!" snarled Zak. "That farm you gave us was no use. The hens don't lay, the cows don't give milk. We've been as poor as beggars since we last saw you."

"Yes and you live here in comfort in our house," added Zik.

"That's not true," said Mathew. "You took my farm from me. You always have the best of everything. I'm only the fool who does all the work."

When the brothers heard this from their quiet brother, they stared at each other with their mouths wide open. "Pinch me, brother – I'm dreaming!" said Zik.

"Pinch me. I'm dreaming too," said Zak. So they pinched each other until it hurt. Then with howls of rage, they tumbled out of the bed and lunged at Mathew. But he stepped nimbly aside and dashed from the room.

Zik and Zak picked up anything they could get their hands on. Mathew dodged cups, plates, firewood - everything that came hurtling after him. Since there was nowhere he could hide safely on the farm, he ran out on to the road and did not stop until he was well away.

"They're g-going to h-hound me all my l-life," he panted, when he stopped to get his breath back. "They'll always want whatever I have."

"Not if you go far enough away," said a familiar chirping voice. Mathew saw beside him the swallow that had helped him years before. Its black, blue and white feathers shone in the moonlight. "Krakov is a fine city," it went on. "Many a time I have perched on its church spires. Go to Krakov, Mathew."

35

"That's where Danuta lives," said Mathew. "How strange that you should say Krakov." But he was talking to himself. The swallow had flown off into the darkness. Mathew considered its advice. Since it had been right about his father's fortune, he decided to go to Krakov.

First, he sold his farm which was not worth much now that his brothers had let it run down. But with what money he had, Mathew went to find Danuta in the city of Krakov.

Several days later, as the bright sun of summer turned to the golden one of autumn, Mathew arrived in Krakov. He had no difficulty in finding Danuta's house; she had described it so often. It was a fine manor house, north of the city.

Danuta was delighted to see him and her father and mother made him very welcome.

"We cannot tell you how grateful we are to you for helping our daughter in her distress," said the mother.

"Danuta is our only child and but for you we might never have seen her again," said the father. Going to a cupboard, he brought out a bag of money. "I wish to return this to you," he said, offering it to Mathew.

"Oh sir, this is not mine – " Mathew began.

"Indeed it is. You will find in there the amount you must have spent on Danuta. The rest is an expression of our immense gratitude." Although Mathew protested, the moneybag was put into his hands.

With this reward for his kindness, Mathew was able to buy another farm. It was a short distance from Danuta's home and a long, long way from Zik and Zak.

In time, Mathew's new farm was flourishing. He was able to buy more and more land until he was a respected country gentleman. Danuta's parents were very impressed with his hard work and readily agreed that he could marry their daughter.

Every year, a swallow came to nest under the roof of their home. Mathew liked to think it was the swallow that had come to him in the past. Perhaps it was, but it did not say so.

Mathew lived a long and happy life with Danuta near the city of Krakov and he never set eyes on his selfish brothers again.

KRYSTA'S MONEYBOX

Krysta lived in a tiny house that was painted bright blue on the outside and all the colours of the rainbow within. It stood for shelter with its back to the tall pine forest. Krysta lived alone, apart from a black cat that followed her everywhere. She had a few hens that gave fresh eggs, a goat that gave fresh milk and she grew her own vegetables on a square patch of ground. Krysta was happy. She thought she had all she needed for a happy life and she was friendly to all who came by.

One year in November, when the first snows of winter had settled deeply on the ground and rested like white clouds on the pine trees, Krysta thought she would spend a few days with her grandmother. It was granny's one hundred and tenth birthday on Christmas Day and she had not been well. Krysta did not make the journey every year since it was a long and dangerous way on foot to the swamplands of the north.

She set about her usual preparations. She made some goat's milk cheese which she hung in muslin on the trees, so that the cheese would dry in the wind. When it was ready, she shaped it into roosters which always pleased her grandmother. Next Krysta baked a special granny cake which needed ten of the freshest eggs from her hens. Then she packed everything into a cloth bag. She drew on her thick felt boots, her sheepskin coat and hat and with a string of dried mushrooms round her neck – granny's favourites – she was ready to go.

She was about to lock up when she remembered her money box. There it was on the dresser where it always stood. It was safe enough as long as she was there, but Krysta knew she could not go on a journey and leave it in sight.

Since there was no safe place to hide it in her house, Krysta decided to bury it in the garden. No one would think of looking there.

She cleared a space in the snow, but when she tried to dig with her spade she found the soil was frozen hard and the spade would not cut into it.

As she stood forlornly wondering what to do, she heard the sound of bagpipes in the distance. Two shepherds came into view on the country road. One was playing the pipes and the other was singing loudly and kicking up his heels.

"Hello there, madam," said the first shepherd as they drew close. "It's not a day for gardening, you know." He pointed to the spade.

"Nobody digs in this weather," said the second shepherd. "Better leave it till the springtime."

Without stopping to think, Krysta explained about the moneybox which was on the ground beside her. Immediately, she regretted her words. These men were strangers to her. They could easily snatch the box and run off with it. She was thinking how silly she was when one of the shepherds said:

"There's no need to hide your money. Why not leave it with the moneylender in the village?"

Krysta did not know there was a moneylender in the village. She hardly ever needed to go there.

"Oh yes, he's got the stoutest locks and bolts I've ever seen," said the second shepherd. "You can't go wrong with him."

"Then that's just what I'll do," said Krysta. She liked the shepherds straightaway and trusted what they said. "How fortunate that we met. Thank you gentlemen and good day."

She folded the moneybox into her shawl and plodded through the snow to the village. The moneylender's shop was dark inside. There was nothing much to see only rows of cupboards, fastened with strong padlocks and bolts. The shopkeeper sat on a high stool behind the counter, scribbling in a ledger.

"Good morning, sir," said Krysta.

"Uh!" said the man gruffly, scarcely looking up.

"I want to leave my moneybox with you while I go on a long journey," said Krysta softly.

At once the man stood up and his eyes glittered. "Ah, you want to *leave* money with me, not borrow it? Oh, with the greatest of pleasure." He was already reaching out for the box.

"It is all I have and if you guard it for me, I will pay you well on my return." Krysta did not like the look of the man, but she did not think she had a choice.

"Rest assured, it is safe with me," said the moneylender, rubbing his fingers together. "Feel free to journey around the world; your money is safe with me. Goodbye! Goodbye! Goodbye!"

Krysta waited until she saw her box safely locked away, then went home to collect her cloth bag and the black cat which sprang up to ride on her shoulder. Together they set off on the long journey to the north.

The weather was sharp with frost. It crisped the top of the snow in spite of a pale sun that sat like an egg-yolk in the grey sky and was no help at all. They left the forest behind and moved on to the wide plain where icy winds cut like razors and the black cat snuggled down inside Krysta's sheepskin coat. Only Krysta's eyes peered out under her fur hat and the sun was her only guide in the vast expanse of gleaming snow.

After many weary days, they came to the edge of a fast-flowing river which had not frozen over. Krysta cupped her hands to her mouth and called across the water. "Yoo-hoo!" She had never learned to yodel like the highlanders who could call across mountains, but "Yoo-hoo!" worked well enough.

From the other side came a faint whistle. A boatman waved a flag before climbing into his rowing-boat. Over he came as he had done before. He rowed Krysta across the water and in return for his help, Krysta gave him two rooster cheeses for Christmas.

"May you have the health and strength to enjoy my cheese," she said.

"And a Merry Christmas to you," said the boatman as they parted.

There was not much further to go after that. Krysta's grandmother lived near one of the wildest forests in the world. It was a place where mist swirled among the massive trees day and night and the cries of bison and boar came eerily through it. This was the part of the journey that Krysta feared most of all, yet none of the powerful animals harmed her. It was as though they knew she was no threat to them.

At last, her grandmother's house came into view and there she was opening the door to welcome her.

"Oh, what a good and thoughtful granddaughter you are," she said in a high, thin voice. "Come in and warm yourself, my dear."

Krysta stayed with her grandmother until New Year's Day, listening to the wonderful stories her granny told about the untamed forest and the strange and gruesome things that rose up out of the swamps. Krysta had heard most of the stories before, but they never ceased to terrify her and make her long for the safety of her own little house by the gentle pine forest.

"Why won't you come and live with me, Granny?" asked Krysta when it was time to go. "My house is warm and we would be together."

Her grandmother's reply was the same as always: "Here I was born and here I stay. Besides, what would I do if I had no fearsome tales to tell? Come back whenever you can and may God go with you."

So Krysta and her cat set off on the weary journey home. The snow was deeper than ever. Sometimes it came almost up to her shoulder. But her nerve did not fail her. So long as the tiniest peep of sun was there or the high, clear sky gave her starlight, Krysta knew exactly in which direction she was going.

When they had returned safely to the little painted house, Krysta lit a big log fire. After a good rest, she went to see the moneylender.

"Good evening," said Krysta politely. "I have come to collect my moneybox please. How much do I owe you?"

"Moneybox? What moneybox?" asked the man cagily.

"My wooden moneybox," said Krysta, "the one that contains all the money I have. I left it with you before Christmas when I went away. Now I am home and I would like to have it back, please."

The shopkeeper pretended to know nothing about it, but Krysta would not be put off.

"It is in that cupboard over there." She indicated the place where she knew it should be.

"Nonsense," said the man. "There's nothing in it." He opened the cupboard which was not locked and it was empty. The moneylender had tricked her.

Krysta's lips began to quiver. "You know you were to guard it for me. Now I have nothing left at all."

But her words went unheeded. "I've never seen you before," lied the man. "Don't try your mischief on me. It's closing time, so off you go and let me lock up."

Krysta saw there was no point in arguing with him. She left the shop and began to trudge desolately along the snowy road. She was so upset she stopped beside a gate to dry her tears. As she looked up at the starry sky, she thought what a sad place the world can be if you are alone. She was still thinking this when she heard the sound of loud singing. It was the two shepherds whom she had met before. Between them they were carrying a large, wooden chest slung on straps from their shoulders. When they saw Krysta they put the chest on the ground and asked what was wrong. Trying to hold back her tears, Krysta told them what had happened.

"It is entirely our fault," said the first shepherd. "We advised you to go to the moneylender."

"Yes," said the second shepherd, "and we will have to think of a way to help you."

"No, I'll never see my money again," sobbed Krysta. "I should have asked him to give me a note for the box, but I did not think."

The shepherds walked off a little way and stood muttering together. They soon came up with an idea.

"Will you do exactly as we say once more?" asked the first shepherd.

"Yes, yes, anything you like," agreed Krysta since she still trusted the shepherds.

"Good," said the second shepherd. "Go back and wait outside the shop until you see us go in. Then you must come in and ask again for your moneybox. If it is still there, you will get it for sure."

Although she knew the shop was closed, Krysta did as she was bid. As she went, she looked back once or twice and was puzzled to see the shepherds bending over the wooden chest which now had its lid open. But she could not tell what they were doing. She stood in a dark corner by the shop, shivering with cold and nerves, and waited.

Snowflakes were silently wafting about when she heard the soft plooff! plooff! of footsteps on the padded ground. It was the shepherds almost bent double with the weight of the chest. Krysta did not think it had seemed so heavy before.

They did not speak or even look in her direction, but banged loudly on the door of the shop. Again and again they knocked and rattled the handle until the moneylender unlocked the door and peered through the chink.

"What's all this banging about for at this time of night?" he asked angrily. "Can't you see the shop's shut? Clear off to your beds, whoever you are!"

"Oh, we can't do that," whispered one of the shepherds. "We daren't take home – er – what we've got in the chest."

"Eh? Why? What do you carry?" inquired the moneylender, his nose now coming round the door.

"Shh!" said the other shepherd. "Don't wake the nation. We don't want anyone to know. There could be robbers about. We've got – "

"No, not a word," cut in the first shepherd. "We promised not to speak of it."

"Ah-ha!" cried the moneylender, already throwing open the door. "You mean – gold? Is it gold?" he chuckled greedily.

"Now you said it, not us," said both of the shepherds together.

At once, the shepherds were ushered into the shop. In the candlelight, they began discussions about depositing the heavily laden chest. It was then that Krysta walked in as she had agreed and stood quietly at the counter. There was a sudden hush as all

three men turned to look at her.

"Attend to this person first, if you please," said one of the shepherds. "Ours is strictly private business, you understand?" He bowed to Krysta and she curtseyed in return.

"I saw the door open as I passed by," she said smiling sweetly. "So I came in again to ask for my moneybox, the one I left with you before Christmas."

The moneylender was plainly impatient and anxious to be rid of her. He went at once to the cupboards on the wall and had no difficulty in producing the moneybox after all.

"Here, here. Take it away. Just go," he said hastily. Without even bothering about payment, he hurried Krysta out of the shop. As she went, she winked at the shepherds and they bowed to the ground.

It was not long before the shepherds caught up with her. They were laughing so much, she could not understand what they were saying.

They all went home and ate hot beef soup and potato cakes. Krysta joined in the laughter when she heard that they had filled the chest with rocks.

"After all," said the first shepherd. "We didn't say we were carrying gold, did we?"

"Not a word about gold passed our lips, that's true," laughed the second shepherd. "The moneylender said 'gold' - miserly fellow."

"But what was in the chest when I saw you?" asked Krysta. "You were not carrying rocks about, were you?"

"No, we were carrying my bagpipes," said the first shepherd. "The chest is a birthday present for my sister and I didn't know where to hide it until Saturday. So two problems are solved at once."

"And if he is nosy enough to look inside," said the second shepherd, "he will not be able to say a word about it."

It was Krysta who had the last word. "The next time I go to see my grandmother, I will leave my moneybox with you. You are my very best friends."

The chest was collected by the shepherds on the Saturday. By Monday, the moneylender's shop was closed and shuttered and he was never seen again.

THE CARPET BAG

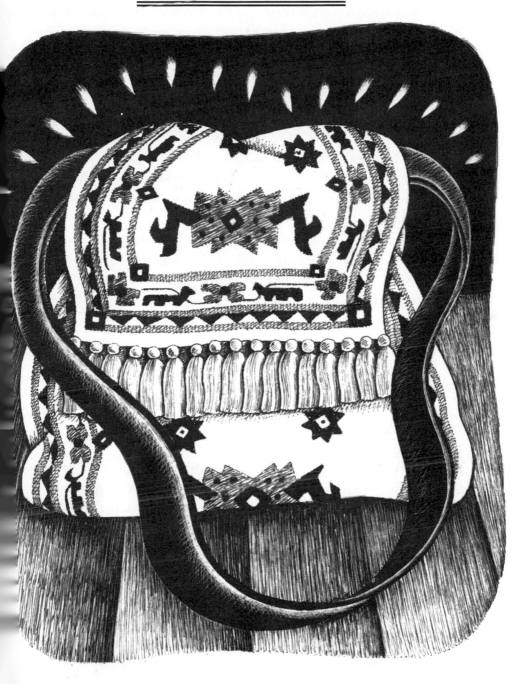

There was once a man who owned an old wooden house. It had belonged to his father, his grandfather and even his great grandfather. When the man became ill and knew that he was dying, he called his two sons to him and asked them not to sell or divide the property. He begged them to stay together and share everything. Although the house was dilapidated and let in mighty draughts, the sons agreed to do as their father said.

After their father's death, Karol and his brother Stash were content to go on living as before. They worked the smallholding which brought them scant income, but they enjoyed each other's company.

Then one day, Karol announced that he intended to marry Krysia, a girl from the nearby village. Although he insisted that they would continue to live as before, Stash decided that he would go and chance his luck in the world.

"After all," he said, "I am as free as air and you will not be alone. It's time I saw what the big world has to offer. It might be a good laugh! Who knows?" It was in his nature always to be optimistic and find a joke wherever he could.

The next morning, Stash prepared to go. He had an old carpet bag which he had made years before from a worn-out rug and into it he put his few possessions.

Karol was sorry to see his younger brother leave but he put on a brave face. "Remember, Stash," he said, "half of this property is yours. Father wanted it so. Come whenever you wish. You'll do well in the world with your quick wit; it'll help you make your fortune. As for me, I'll plod on here in my own slow way. Call me tortoise, if you like."

Stash did not call his brother tortoise, but gave him a wide smile and a hearty slap on the back. Swinging his carpet bag over his shoulder, he walked merrily along the road, whistling.

By nightfall, Stash was tired and hungry. He had eaten nothing since breakfast. When he came to a mill that was set back in a clover field, he thought he might be given shelter for the night.

The miller was away on business, but his wife Anna said she did not mind if Stash spent the night in the grain loft. She gave him a bundle of fresh hay to spread on the floor and Stash lay down expecting to get a good night's sleep.

He had just dozed off when he was awakened by the sound of jovial voices and the clinking of glasses, not to mention a glorious smell of food. It was Anna and her young brother in the room below. Now Stash did not know it, but this young man was a penniless painter and when the miller had offered him a job at the mill – a partnership! – the young man had refused. The angry miller had told him not to show his face at the mill again until he had a decent job. So it had been until this particular evening, which was the young man's birthday and he had just sold his first painting.

Looking through the space between the floorboards, Stash saw a table on which were a roast chicken, a bottle of wine and cheese and biscuits.

"This *is* a surprise," Anna was saying. "Fancy bringing your own food on your birthday. Well, here's to the start of better days, Premko. You were never meant to be a miller. Happy birthday, my dear."

The brother and sister drank more toasts to each other and they were about to eat when they heard the sound of a cart drawing up outside.

"Merciful goodness!" cried Anna. "It's my husband! He said he wouldn't be back until tomorrow. We'd better hide the food, quickly."

They rushed about in a panic. They jammed the chicken and the bottle of wine behind the dresser and Premko pushed the cheese and biscuits under the eiderdown which had just been re-stuffed and was airing by the fire.

"But what about me?" whispered Premko. "He mustn't find me here. He hates painters."

"Hurry," urged his sister. "There's a barrel of feathers in the storeroom. Get into it and don't move until I say so."

The terrified brother rushed into the darkened storeroom and jumped into a barrel of tar by mistake. He soon climbed out and dived headfirst into the barrel of eider feathers, just as the miller opened the door.

All this was seen by Stash who tried to hide his laughter in the hay.

"Here comes a hu-u-ungry man, my little bird," said the miller, removing his coat and tossing his hat at a peg. "And, I declare, I smell roast chicken for dinner. Am I right, my pet?"

"I think you only smell pickled herrings, my love," replied Anna. "Remember, I was not expecting you until tomorrow."

The miller looked puzzled. "Pickled herrings? But I am sure I smell roast chicken," he said, sniffing and looking about.

"Perhaps you smell the eider feathers airing at the fire," smiled Anna, pecking him on the cheek. "Come and have your supper."

The perplexed miller sat down to his cold herrings without fathoming how he could mistake the feathers in his eiderdown for a roast chicken. Meanwhile in the loft, Stash stretched out and tried to get back to sleep but his foot accidentally knocked over a wooden stool.

"What's that noise?" demanded the miller, looking upwards.

"Oh, I forgot. It's a traveller. I said he could spend the night in the loft," said Anna, not quite sure if it was in fact her brother falling out of the barrel.

Since Stash was wide awake and hungry as a hunter, even half a cold herring seemed like a banquet to him. So he climbed down from the loft and introduced himself. At once, the miller observed the carpet bag which Stash held in front of him.

"That's a fine looking bag you've got there, young man," he said.

Stash, in his quick-witted way, said instantly: "Oh it's a very fine bag indeed and a rare one too." He stroked the bag, holding it close to his chest.

"How so?" asked the miller.

"Because it's a divining bag," said Stash in a hushed voice.

"A divining bag?" repeated the miller.

"That's right, a divining bag. It finds things. If I give it a quick squeeze, it will find things in the most unlikely places."

"Bah! What rubbish! You take me for a fool," snapped the miller pushing a whole herring into his mouth, while Stash's mouth watered.

Stash, with a mischievous smile, slipped the bag under one arm and gave it a quick squeeze. "Ah-ha!" he cried. "You see, it detects something already. Cheep-cheep-cheep-a-doodle-doo! It says there's a roast chicken and a bottle of wine behind the dresser."

"I doubt that," said the miller, rising from his chair. "But let's have a look." He peered behind the dresser and drew out the chicken and the bottle of wine. "I don't believe it!" he protested, while staring hard at the evidence.

No sooner had the miller put the food on the table, when Stash called out: "Wait, wait! There's something else. It says – why it says you've got cheese and biscuits under your eiderdown."

"Cheese and biscuits … under my eider … ?" The miller, almost overcome with astonishment, lifted the corner of the eiderdown (still airing by the fire) and beheld the cheese and biscuits. By this time, Anna was thoroughly alarmed that her brother might be discovered. She slipped out of the room, while Stash and the miller sat down to enjoy an excellent dinner.

As he ate and drank, the miller could hardly take his eyes from the carpet bag. "Oh what a gem of a bag!" he said from time to time. "What wouldn't I give to have a bag like that?"

"Ah, but such a bag is not easy to come by," said Stash, finishing his last glass of wine. "This could be the only one of its kind left in the world."

"And how *did* you come by it?" asked the miller suspiciously. "You don't look like a wealthy man."

"It's been in my family for generations," said Stash. "But where it came from originally, I couldn't say." He hoped he could now get to sleep for what was left of the night, but the miller had other ideas.

"Why not give it one more go," the miller said eagerly. "Go on, in payment for your night's lodging. Then we'll go to bed."

Stash considered for a moment. It was true he had benefited from a delicious dinner and he was anxious to get to sleep. "All right then," he said. "Only one more time though. We mustn't wear the bag out. Are you ready?"

"Yes, yes!" cried the miller. "Go on, go on."

Stash put the bag under his arm once more and gave it another squeeze. "Oooooh! Oooooh! You're not going to like this one," he said cautiously. "It says - it says -". The miller's eyes, ears and mouth were wide open in anticipation. "It says there's a monster in your storeroom, at this very minute."

"A monster in my storeroom, this very minute?" The miller seemed to like repeating everything he heard. "Then we'll get sticks and knock it out of there, this very minute!" he fumed. He rushed away for sticks and both he and Stash crept towards the storeroom. Meanwhile the "monster", having heard it had been discovered, had come out of the barrel of feathers, but could get no further.

The quaking monster-brother took a good whacking, protesting to the heavens with howls of sorrow, until he was saved by his sister opening the door at the back. He ran off across the clover field and into the night.

Though both men were exhausted after truly exciting entertainment, the miller was still mesmerised by the unique divining bag. He said he must have it and would pay Stash handsomely if he were willing to part with it. Stash, who could hardly keep his eyes open, agreed to let the miller have the bag.

"But I don't want any money for it," he said, quite honestly. "You can have it as a present. You have been very kind to me. It's the least I can do." So the miller took possession of the bag and at last they both went to sleep.

When Stash rose in the morning, Anna came to him and said: "Please don't leave that bag with my husband. He was very unkind to my brother and he's a good boy. I'll give you three gold pieces if you'll take it away."

Stash refused to take her money, but he gave her a piece of advice. "I cannot take the bag away; I have given it to the miller," he said. "But the bag will lose all its power if you make a few holes in it. It will then be like any other bag."

After a good breakfast of pork and beans, provided by the grateful Anna, Stash thanked them both for their hospitality. Then he went on his way, he knew not where.

An hour or so later, when he put his hands in his pockets, Stash found: six gold pieces in one pocket and three gold pieces in the other. Somehow the miller and Anna had managed to pay him for the old, worn-out bag which he had only used as a joke.

Since he could not return the gold pieces without revealing the true events of the night before, Stash bought himself a house with the money. It was almost identical to that of his father's, only in first-rate condition.

When he had it all in good order, he invited Karol and Krysia to come and visit him. They were delighted to see that Stash had done so well. When he explained where his wealth had come from, it gave Karol and Krysia an idea.

"We could do with a bit of money," said Karol. "I think the old house won't last much longer."

"That's true," said Krysia. "I think I'll make a carpet bag and we'll see if it brings us some good luck."

When they went home, Krysia cut up an old rug and made a carpet bag exactly as Stash had done many years before. And Karol, although he was not a travelling man, agreed to go and see if he could make his fortune.

He rolled along the road in his cart, taking an unfamiliar route. After a time, the pony ambled through a quiet village. It passed a clover field where a narrow lane led to a mill house and Karol thought this might be a good place to start. Trying to look confident, which was not his usual demeanour, he knocked on the door of the house while the pony cropped the clover.

Unfortunately, this was the very mill in which his brother Stash had spent the night.

"I wonder, would you like to buy a rare divining bag?" he asked the miller who opened the door.

"A rare divining bag, you say?" repeated the miller, his eyes almost starting from his head.

Karol nodded, quite taken aback by the miller's ferocious face.

"Is that so! Then just stand where you are," commanded the miller. "We'll be with you in one moment."

He hurried away and in four or five moments, an angry crowd from the village advanced on Karol, carrying sticks and all kinds of other things.

"It's another one of those carpetbaggers," the miller was roaring. "Come on boys, let's get him! I've had enough of this."

Karol did not wait to hear more. Petrified, he hurled himself into his cart, set the pony at a gallop and was gone as fast as his cart could carry him. He was so alarmed, he did not dare call at another house. Instead, he drove on, letting the pony wander where it chose.

When the pony was tired, they stopped to rest in an empty barn. It was only then that Karol realised he had left the carpet bag on the step of the mill house. But it mattered little; he knew he never wanted to see it again. Before long, he fell into a troubled sleep.

He woke later to find a menacing sky closing in, with purple storm clouds swirling so low they seemed to devour the trees.

That night, one of the fiercest thunderstorms in many years raged across the countryside. Karol saw the sky lit up with jagged lightning and trees and bushes whipped and uprooted by the screaming gale. Raindrops the size of chestnuts bombarded the earth and flattened the fragile crops. He was glad of a dry roof over his head. By the time dawn spread upwards over the distant mountains, the storm had spent its force.

Karol harnessed the pony and set off for home. But when he reached the plot of land on which the old wooden house had stood, the old wooden house was no longer there. Strewn across the flooded land was the debris – bits and pieces of painted wood and broken furniture, which he recognised only too well. There was no sign of Krysia. Karol searched for her and called her name, but there was no reply.

With a heavy heart, he drove on to his brother's house. When it came into view, his spirits rose at the sight of Krysia and Stash at the window, awaiting him. Stash explained how he had gone to the old house at the height of the storm and found Krysia alone.

He had arrived just in time before the building had been washed away.

There was much rejoicing that all three of them were safely together again and in a house so much like the one which they had lost. Soon it was like old times – the brothers were content to work the smallholding and they were happy in each other's company. It pleased Karol and Stash to know that they had not broken their promise to their father. After all, they had not sold the old wooden house – it had simply floated away.

Oh, and on the subject of carpet bags, not a word was ever said again.